I Don't Like
Spiders
But They Seem
To Like Me

No
Spiders

by
Pat Nicholson
Illustrations by MikeMotz.com

"To my beautiful, special family:
Kelly, Kim, Sean, Michael and Glenn.
With all my love, I thank you."

Story by Pat Nicholson
Illustrations by MikeMotz.com

ISBN: 1470024659
EAN-13: 978-1470024659

Printed in the U.S.A.

I Don't Like
Spiders
But They Seem
To Like Me

For Grace, Taylor and Isaiah,

Happy Reading!

:) Pat

March 20, 2012

I don't like spiders,

but they seem
to like me.

Everywhere I go...

they just seem to be.

In Summer, in Spring,
in Winter or Fall...

I just can't seem
to get a break
at all.

Like when I'm lying on the floor
just reading my book,

something moves on
the ceiling...
causing me to look.

Or when I go to the fridge
just to get some tasty food,
here comes another one again...

Sometimes, there I am all comfy in my bed...

when suddenly I see
something dangling over my head.

or go running
for a broom...

but why, oh why,
do spiders seem to love my room?

I try my best to ignore them—
pretend they're just
not there...

Of course I would never
hurt them…
I'll always let them be,

Instead, they come inside the house and find a cozy spot.

I guess
I understand
that part...

but then again...

MAYBE NOT!!!!!

face approached her belly, her breasts. She felt on her dress, on her bodice, the warmth of his breath while he continued to speak, though she could not hear what he was saying, merely the hissing of words repeating the same things, the whistling of her first name, spoken in low, insistent tones, with sighs and silences.

"Pretty legs, pretty legs," said the voice, and Hyangsu wondered if he was talking about her, about her legs, her body. Now she looked at him and saw little drops of sweat beading on his forehead, where the hair had receded, and over his bushy eyebrows. She saw the tops of his eyelids, somewhat gray and wrinkled, and the rest of his body, the white shirt crumpled at the collar, the arms leaning on the table, and the hands advancing, two dark, muscular animals, traversed on the backs by veins in the shape of tree branches. The hands that clasped her legs, then slowly slid upwards, towards the forbidden places.

I stopped. I looked at Salome. Her head was leaning a little to one side, as if her neck did not have enough strength to hold it straight. The skin of her face was